THE WEEBIE ZONE #2

Sing, Elvis, Sing !

by Stephanie Spinner
and Ellen Weiss

illustrated by Steve Björkman

HarperTrophy
A Division of HarperCollins*Publishers*

For Ginger, Hugo, and Beau
—S.S.

For Michael
—S.B.

SING, ELVIS, SING!
Text copyright © 1996 by Stephanie Spinner and Ellen Weiss
Illustrations © 1996 by Steve Björkman
Printed in the
United States of America. For information address HarperCollins Children's Books, a
division of HarperCollins Publishers,
10 East 53rd Street, New York, NY 10022.

Library of Congress Cataloging-in-Publication Data
Spinner, Stephanie.
  Sing, Elvis, sing! / by Stephanie Spinner and Ellen Weiss ; illustrated by Steve
Björkman.
    p.   cm. — (The Weebie zone)
  Summary: While visiting his aunt in Atlanta, Garth and his pet gerbil plan an
unusual event which restores her dog, Elvis, to his former frisky self.
  ISBN 0-06-027337-2 (lib. bdg.). — ISBN 0-06-442032-9 (pbk.)
  [1. Aunts—Fiction. 2. Dogs—Fiction. 3. Gerbils—Fiction.] I. Weiss, Ellen,
date. II. Björkman, Steve, ill. III. Title. IV. Series: Spinner, Stephanie. Weebie
zone.
PZ7.S7567Si 1996   95-51257
[Fic]—dc20   CIP
                                                                          AC

1 2 3 4 5 6 7 8 9 10
❖
First Edition

Contents

CHAPTER ONE

··

Going South

"**B**ut Mom, I thought I could stay home for the rest of the summer!" Garth Hunter kicked a rock down the street. His mother had just told him that he was going to spend part of August in Georgia with his aunt.

"I know we said that." Mrs. Hunter loaded the last bag of groceries into the car. "But that was before we got all that money from Great-Great-Uncle Bill." She slammed the trunk.

"Well, who was he anyway?" asked Garth.

"Yeah, who *was* he?" squeaked Weebie from Garth's waist pack. Garth ignored him.

"I'm not quite sure," replied his mother. "I never met him. I think he was my mother's stepfather's uncle. But I guess he knew who we were. He left us a nice little bit of money, just enough for a vacation for your father and me."

Garth kicked another rock down the street.

"Now, Garth," she said. "You know your father and I haven't had a vacation for three years. I've been working way too hard, and getting my Ph.D. at the same time, and it's been rough. We *need* some time off, just the two of us. Besides, we'll come home all mellow and happy. That'll make you happy, won't it?"

"I guess so," Garth admitted.

"And you know you'll have fun at Aunt Barb's. You always have fun down there."

It was true. If he had to be packed off to a relative, Aunt Barb was definitely the one. She was cool.

"Aunt Barb! Aunt Barb!" chanted Weebie. "Let's go!"

Garth used a finger to push Weebie's head back down into the waist pack. He was glad he was the only one who could understand what Weebie was saying. All his mother could hear was tiny gerbil squeaks.

"So are we okay on this?" she asked.

"Yeah," said Garth. "We're okay."

"Thanks for understanding, honey," said his mother, ruffling his hair. "I really appreciate it."

They got into the car and headed home from the supermarket.

"So, big guy, what's the story on Aunt Barb?" asked Weebie as they drove.

Garth didn't answer. He couldn't, and Weebie knew it. The gerbil was just teasing him. There was no way Garth could talk to him while Mrs. Hunter was around.

As if his mother could deal with the New Garth—the boy who could talk to animals! Sure. He could just imagine trying to explain it to her: "See, Mom, after I forgot to feed Weebie once too often, he bit me. And after that, I could understand him. Now we talk all the time."

Garth stole a glance at his mother. She was smart and understanding, but she'd never buy it. He could hardly believe it himself.

"Does Aunt Barb still have that dog?" he asked.

"Elvis? I think so. I can't imagine Barb without him."

Well, that would be fun, thought Garth.

Elvis was a great dog, a big, floppy brown-and-white hound with a sweet face. He loved to play.

Garth wondered if he would be able to talk to Elvis.

Now there was a thought. Suddenly his summer looked a lot more interesting.

Garth peered out of the little window as the plane approached Atlanta. He could just see the tall buildings of the city through the clouds. He was excited. He had never flown alone before.

His parents had been about fifty times more nervous than he was at the airport. His father had kept going to the check-in desk to make sure the flight attendants would be nice to Garth during the trip. His mother had checked the contents of his duffel bag three times. Yes, his money was tucked away inside. Yes, his return ticket to Connecticut was with it. And yes, the present for Aunt Barb was at the bottom of the bag.

His parents had stood in the window at the departure gate, waving hard as the plane took off. In a flash they were tiny specks. That was barely two hours ago. Now here he was, all alone in another part of the country, where people spoke with a whole different accent.

Bing! The Fasten Seat Belt sign lit up, startling him.

"What was that?" squeaked Weebie from Garth's waist pack.

"I think it means we're landing," said Garth. He fastened his seat belt.

"OW! You squished me! Watch it!"

"Sorry." Very gently, Garth rearranged Weebie. Then he watched, fascinated, as the ground came rushing toward them. It was awesome, almost like being in a jet-powered elevator. He gave a little bounce of excitement in his seat.

"I want to see! I want to see!" called Weebie. Garth was glad he had the double seat to himself, and that the flight was almost empty. He looked around to make sure nobody was watching. Then he took Weebie out of his waist pack and lifted him to the window.

"Wow!" said Weebie, whiskers twitching. Garth could feel his tiny heart beating about ten thousand times a second.

And then they were on the ground.

When the plane pulled up to the gate, Garth put Weebie away and got his duffel bag down from the overhead compartment. He picked it up and headed for the door.

"Hold on there, Mr. Garth Hunter," said the

flight attendant, whose name tag said "Charlene." She had long blond curls and a big smile, and had given him five bags of peanuts with his apple juice. "I have to make sure your party meets you, honey. And I have to give you these."

Smiling widely, she produced a silvery wing-shaped pin. "Where do you want your wings, sweetheart?" she asked. "On your li'l fanny pack?" She started to stick the pin into Garth's waist pack.

There was a tiny alarmed shriek from inside it.

"No! That's okay," Garth said quickly. "I'll just save them." He took the pin from her and stuck it in his jeans pocket.

A moment later they were inside the Atlanta airport. There were lots of people at the gate. Would he recognize Aunt Barb? It had been at least two years since he'd seen her.

"You're meeting your aunt, right, honey?" asked Charlene. "Is that her?" She indicated a woman in a flowered dress and high heels.

"No," said Garth, looking around. He spotted her right away. "That's my aunt," he said, pointing her out.

Charlene stared. "You mean the woman with the tattoo?"

Garth nodded. Aunt Barb wore a sleeveless denim shirt, which made it hard to miss the blue lightning bolt on her arm. Her dark curly hair, longer than Garth remembered it, was tied back with a pink bandanna. Her jeans were black, with legs as long and skinny as licorice sticks, and her pointy-toed cowboy boots were red.

"Yoo-hoo!" she called, waving. "Garth! Over here!"

Charlene handed Garth over quickly. She was gone before Aunt Barb had even finished her hello hug. The hug went on for a long time, with pats and rubs and shoulder squeezes. Finally it was over, and Aunt Barb stood back.

"Let me take a good look at you," she said, grinning. "Whooee, you have *grown*! You'll be as tall as me soon!"

Garth blushed. His aunt always paid him lots of compliments. It was embarrassing, but he liked it.

She picked up his duffel. "You still like barbecued chicken, à la Barb?"

Garth nodded. His aunt's barbecued chicken was practically the best thing he'd ever tasted.

"Good!" she said. "The barbecue's heatin' up right now. Let's hustle." She swung the duffel over her shoulder and started off down the corridor, moving so fast that Garth had to run to keep up with her.

As he hurried along, he wondered again how she and his mother could be sisters. They were so different! His mother loved to read and discuss things. She wrote papers and worked on committees. Her idea of a great time was talking to people about their problems, which was why she was studying to be a psychologist. She had no interest in sports and started yawning when Garth and his dad talked about baseball. As for exercise, she hated it. "Mental fitness!" she'd say. "That's what counts!"

Aunt Barb, on the other hand, said she got itchy if she stayed indoors too long, which was why she worked for the post office. She delivered mail. The only thing she ever read, as far as Garth knew, was truck magazines. She liked to rebuild old trucks. Her latest was a cherry-

red 1955 Ford pickup. She'd sent them pictures of it on her last Christmas card.

Garth knew Aunt Barb and his mother loved each other a lot. Still, he couldn't help thinking there'd been a mix-up at the hospital when Aunt Barb was born. Somewhere out there, he suspected, was a studious woman with dangling earrings who'd been taken away by the wrong parents. His real aunt.

Meanwhile, Aunt Barb was a great substitute.

They walked through blazing heat into a huge covered parking lot. After passing rows and rows of cars, Garth finally spotted it—Aunt Barb's bright-red truck. Elvis was in the passenger seat, looking out the window.

Aunt Barb unlocked the doors. She dropped Garth's duffel in the back of the truck and climbed into the driver's seat.

Garth sat down next to the dog.

"Well, if it isn't Garth," said Elvis.

CHAPTER TWO

All Frisked Out

The freeway took them through the city, with its new skyscrapers, and out past the suburbs. Soon they were in the country. Here it was wide open and green, and much emptier than Connecticut. And much hotter.

"When we drive out here after this," said Aunt Barb, "I'll let you ride in back with Elvis if you want."

"Wow!" squeaked Weebie.

"Wow!" echoed Garth. "Thanks!" He'd never been allowed before, and he knew it would be fun. As they chugged along, other drivers turned to watch them. Some smiled and beeped a greeting. It was all because of Aunt

Barb's truck, which was red and as shiny as patent leather. Its big round headlights and curving chrome fenders made it look as if it were smiling, almost like a cartoon truck.

Aunt Barb was really proud of it.

Garth could tell when they reached his aunt's town. Every single person on the street waved to her, and she waved back.

"Got your nephew there?" asked the man who filled up their tank in front of the country store.

"Sure do," said Aunt Barb proudly. "His name's Garth."

"Pleased to meet you, Garth," said the man. He reached into the cab to shake Garth's hand.

They headed down the street and out of town. "They're so friendly here," said Garth, as a woman and two kids waved at them. "I mean, people are nice in Connecticut, but not *this* nice."

"That's Georgia for you," said Aunt Barb. "Not a bad old place."

They drove down roads that got narrower, bumpier, and dustier, until they reached a mailbox standing under a giant sunflower. Then they turned into Aunt Barb's front yard.

The house was just as Garth remembered it—white wood, gray shutters, a big rickety front porch with pots of flowers and a wooden swing.

There were other things to swing from, too. A big old tire dangling from a tree. A striped hammock with a pillow in it.

"I like it here!" chirped Weebie.

Down a little hill was the pond, and above the pond was a knotted rope tied to a tree branch. You could use the rope to swing right out over the pond and let go, cannonballing into the water. Garth had forgotten about that.

"Like to help me set the table?" asked his aunt. "Or would you like to go for a swim first?"

"I'll swim, if that's okay," said Garth.

"Course it's okay," she said. "Go ahead. And take Elvis with you. He needs a little fun." She picked up Garth's duffel and carried it into the house.

"C'mon, Elvis," said Garth.

The dog followed him down to the water's edge. He settled beneath a tree and watched as Garth took Weebie out of his pack.

"Who's this?" asked Elvis. His smooth, low-pitched voice reminded Garth of a cello.

"This is Weebie," said Garth. "Do you like gerbils?"

"Sure," said Elvis. He sighed heavily. "No problem."

Garth stripped down to his shorts and folded his clothes on the grass. "Want to swim?" he asked the dog.

"No thanks," said Elvis, resting his head on his paws. "I'll just lie here."

Garth scooped Weebie up and waded into the water with him.

"Eek!" squeaked Weebie. "What are you doing?"

"We're going for a swim," said Garth.

"Gerbils don't swim!" protested Weebie.

"Don't worry—I won't drop you. It'll be fun."

"Be careful!" said Weebie. "If you kill me, I'll be really mad at you."

Garth laughed. The water was cool and wonderful. He ducked, holding Weebie up so he wouldn't get wet. "Sure you don't want to come in?" he called softly to Elvis. "It's great in here. You'll cool right off."

"No thanks," said Elvis. "Really."

"Are you okay?" asked Garth. "You used to be so frisky. Is anything wrong?"

"I guess I'm all frisked out," said Elvis with another sigh. He raised his head and looked at Garth with just a little bit of curiosity. "How come you can talk to me, anyway?"

"It's all Weebie's fault," said Garth. He told Elvis about taking Weebie home from school for the summer, and forgetting to feed him, and how Weebie bit him. "And after that I could talk to him, and to other animals, too," Garth told Elvis. "Amazing, huh?"

"I guess I'd be excited about this, if I were getting excited about anything," said Elvis. "But I'm not. So I won't." He put his head down again.

"Maybe I can help—" Garth began, but at that moment Aunt Barb called him for dinner. "Let's go," said Garth. "Maybe we can talk about what's bothering you later." Then he got his first whiff of barbecue. It was so delicious that he forgot Elvis' problems and broke into a run. Three seconds later he was at the house.

Once inside, he saw that Aunt Barb had

company. Two men and a woman were playing cards at the table.

"Go fish!" exclaimed one of the men. He was thin and balding, and wore a T-shirt that said:

KISS ME

I'M

HUNGARIAN

"Go fish yourself," said the woman, who had spiky red hair and glasses with sparkly stones in them.

The second man was short and had gigantic muscles. Suddenly he stood. "I'm not playing with y'all if you're gonna cheat!" he announced.

A noisy squabble broke out immediately.

When she saw Garth, Aunt Barb walked over to him and put her arm around his shoulders. "Hey! You guys!" she called. "Hey!" They didn't even hear her. She put two fingers up to her mouth and let out an earsplitting whistle.

That got their attention.

"I want you to meet somebody," she told them. "This is my nephew, Garth, from Connecticut. Don't be mean or rude to him, hear? He's my favorite nephew."

Garth smiled. He was her only nephew.

"These are my friends from the United States Postal Service," Aunt Barb told him. "The one with the muscles is Arthur. He's a mail sorter. Betty there is a mail carrier, like me. And Attila hides behind the Certified Mail window. Nobody knows what he does."

"Hi," said Garth.

"Want to play go fish with us?" asked Arthur.

"Forget about cards," said Aunt Barb. "You all cheat, and besides, it's time for supper."

They had the table cleared and set before she finished the sentence. Then they all carried the food over, sat down, and dug in. There was barbecued chicken, corn on the cob, fried tomatoes, pickled peppers, biscuits, and turnip greens. Garth couldn't believe it. It was like Thanksgiving in August.

"This chicken is unbelievable," said Attila. "As usual."

"Thanks for cooking this great meal for us," said Betty. "If I was home, I'd be having limeade and Twinkies. That's what I always eat for dinner." She peered at an ear of corn as if trying to figure out what it was.

"Well," said Aunt Barb, "since I split up with Byron, it's kind of lonely around here at mealtimes. I like to cook, but I can't do it just for myself. So I'm glad to have you."

"Byron?" said Garth. "Who's Byron?"

"He was my boyfriend, honey. We split up a few weeks ago."

"Byron was no bargain," said Arthur. "He just sat around the house watching television and eating Barb's food. Never helped with a single thing."

"Sounds a lot like you, Arthur," said Betty, winking at Garth.

Arthur looked offended. "I fully intend to help with the dishes—" he began.

"Great idea!" said Aunt Barb.

"—but first Garth has to tell us about Connecticut."

As they ate, Garth told everyone about his parents, his school, and his friends. Then he took Weebie out of his pack and showed him around.

"Oooh! Cute!" exclaimed Betty.

"Looks smart as anything," said Attila.

If they only knew, thought Garth.

Weebie scampered around the table, doing his I'm-so-adorable act. Aunt Barb gave him a niblet of corn and he ate it daintily, holding it in his little paws.

"We'll have to fix him up with a box in your

room," said Garth's aunt.

"Great!" said Garth. "It doesn't have to be anything fancy, though."

"Hey!" said Weebie.

"Isn't he adorable!" said Betty. "Listen to that little squeak!"

"Oh, brother," said Elvis, who was stationed next to Aunt Barb's chair.

"Elvis, honey!" Aunt Barb said to her dog. "I forgot about you, didn't I?" She pulled a piece of chicken off a drumstick and gave it to him.

"You shouldn't feed him from the table, you know," said Arthur.

"Maybe not," said Aunt Barb, "but he's been so depressed lately. I have a terrible feeling it's because Byron is gone. He really liked Byron."

"Byron was okay but clueless," Elvis told Garth. "I followed him around to make sure he didn't get into trouble."

"There, there, boy," said Aunt Barb, scratching Elvis behind the ears. "We'll both get over Byron. It'll just take time."

"Well, better clean up," said Arthur, standing and stretching. "It's almost time for the big game."

Sing, Elvis, Sing!

Everybody helped clean up. Garth tackled the pots and pans. Weebie sat on the counter nearby watching. Every now and then he'd say, "Missed a spot!" and Garth would flick some water at him.

After about fifteen minutes, Arthur called them, and they all raced into the living room. It was the Atlanta Braves and the New York Mets.

"Are you a Mets fan?" Attila asked Garth.

"No, I root for the Red Sox," said Garth.

"Barb is a fanatical Braves fan," said Betty. "Have you ever seen her prize possession?"

Garth shook his head.

Aunt Barb took something down from a

bookshelf and tossed it to him. It was a baseball. Signed by Chipper Jones.

"Yow!" said Garth.

"I caught this ball," his aunt told him
proudly. "Chipper hit it and I caught it."

"You caught it because you threw yourself

on top of me," groused Arthur. "That should have been my ball."

"You just weren't fast enough, Arthur," said Aunt Barb, grinning.

"Okay, hush up, everybody," said Attila. "Time for the national anthem."

Arthur and Attila stood up and slapped their hands over their hearts as the first notes of the anthem played. A big, bearded man holding a white handkerchief stepped up to home plate and began to sing. He made "The Star-Spangled Banner" sound like *opera*! Garth thought it was weird.

"I can do better than that," muttered Elvis from under the coffee table. "A lot better."

"You can?" asked Garth.

Aunt Barb looked at him. "What?" she asked.

"Oh, nothing," said Garth. "Just clearing my throat."

The singer finished up. "Play ball!" cried the umpire.

While they waited for the first pitch, Betty turned to Garth. "I'll bet you've never heard Elvis sing the anthem, have you?"

"He hasn't," said Aunt Barb. "But he should. Elvis, sing the anthem for Garth, why don't you? Come on, sugar." She hummed the first few notes coaxingly.

Elvis just looked at her from under his eyebrows.

"Can you really sing?" Weebie asked the dog.

"Yes," said Elvis. "Though a lot of good it does me."

"Elvis, is your tummy bothering you?" asked Aunt Barb.

Elvis just put his head down on his front paws.

"Come on, Elvis," said Attila. "Sing the anthem for Garth."

Elvis looked miserable. "She wants to know what my problem is?" he said to Garth. "She wants to know why I'm depressed? Well, *this* is my problem," he said.

Garth wasn't sure he understood what Elvis meant.

"We have to talk to him alone," Weebie squeaked quietly.

Garth thought for a moment. Then he turned to his aunt. "Do you think I could take Elvis into the kitchen and give him a biscuit?" he asked her. "Maybe then he'll feel more like singing."

"Sure, honey, that's fine." The first batter was up, and her eyes were glued to the set.

Garth, holding Weebie, led Elvis into the kitchen. They waited until the swinging door closed behind them. Then Garth sat down on the floor next to the dog. "What's bugging you?" he asked.

"Yeah, tell us," squeaked Weebie. "Maybe we can help you."

"It's this anthem thing," said Elvis. "I sing it, and they treat me like a toy. They don't understand—I'm an artist! I have a *gift*! And it's wasted!"

"If I were a person," he continued, "they'd ask me to open a Braves game in a minute. But no! I'm a dog. And nobody takes me seriously!" Elvis was so upset, he was almost howling.

"Whoa!" said Garth. "You mean it, don't you?"

"Yes, I mean it," said Elvis. "When Barb is at work, I practice at least two hours a day."

"Smokin' cedar chips!" said Weebie. "I'm impressed!"

"Elvis," said Garth, "would you sing the anthem for me? Just so I can hear it? I promise I'll be respectful."

"I'd really like to hear it, too," said Weebie.

Elvis thought about it. "I guess so," he said finally. "Later."

"Thanks," said Garth. They all went back into the living room and settled down again. Garth was hoping that someone would ask Elvis to sing during the commercial break. Sure enough, Arthur did.

"Hey," he said to Elvis. "How 'bout singin' for us, boy?"

"I hate when he calls me 'boy,'" said Elvis. "Doesn't he know it's insulting?"

"Maybe he needs a little coaxing," said Aunt Barb. Elvis was lying under the coffee table, so she got down on her hands and knees next to him. "Elvis, honey," she crooned. "Would you sing for Garth? Pretty please?"

Elvis sighed and came out from under the table. He sat down right next to the television and looked at Aunt Barb. She picked up a pitch pipe and blew an E for him to start on.

His head went back. His eyes closed.

And then he sang:

"Ow ow ow ow ow owww,
Ow ow ow ow ow *oww,*
Ow ow owww
Ow ow owww,
Ow ow ow wow wow wow wow . . . "

Garth's mouth dropped open. Elvis was good! He had perfect timing and perfect pitch. He *was* better than the opera singer. And he was a *dog*!

When Elvis finished, everyone clapped. "Isn't he great?" said Aunt Barb. "Beats me how he learned it. And he just seems to get better and better."

Garth nodded, speechless. Elvis let out one last, windy sigh and lay back down under the coffee table. Garth lay down next to him. Once everyone was watching the game again, he leaned over as if to scratch Elvis' ears.

"Elvis," he whispered, "I'm going to fix it so you can open up a Braves game. I don't know how, but I will."

"And I'm going to help," vowed Weebie. "Gerbil's honor."

....

A Surprise Visitor

The next morning everyone had cleared out of Aunt Barb's house except Attila. He was still asleep on the sofa when Garth, Weebie, and Aunt Barb came down for breakfast.

"Up, up, up!" Aunt Barb yodeled, right in his ear. Attila bolted upright, blinking.

"Where am I?" he asked the room.

"You're at my house," said Aunt Barb. "The Braves lost last night, remember? And you're late for work."

"Omigosh!" cried Attila, leaping off the sofa and running out the door. It slammed behind him.

"You'd think I was their mother," Aunt Barb said to Garth. She opened the refrigerator and began pulling things out of it—eggs, blueberries, butter, milk, coffee.

"Don't you have to go to work too?" he asked.

"With you here?" she said. "No way. I'm on vacation! You and I are going to have some *fun!*"

"Thanks, Aunt Barb." Garth was pleased.

"Don't mention it, honey," she said. "Now let's have some breakfast. We've got a big day ahead of us."

Aunt Barb got busy making coffee and blueberry pancakes. She brought the pancakes to the table warm, buttered, and sprinkled with powdered sugar. Even though he was still full from dinner, Garth managed to eat a few. They were delicious.

"At eleven o'clock," his aunt told him, "we have an appointment."

"An appointment?" Garth didn't like that word. It usually meant something bad, like getting a shot or a filling.

"Yes," said his aunt. "At eleven we are going to call on Miss Ophelia Latouche. You and I and Elvis, that is. Weebie can come too, if you want.

I notice you like to carry him around." She smiled at Weebie, who was in Garth's shirt pocket this morning. He wiggled his whiskers at her.

"Ophelia LaWho?" asked Garth.

"Latouche," said his aunt. "The animal psychic. She's famous. People come to see her from all over the country."

"What's an animal psychic?"

"She's supposed to be able to tell what animals are thinking," said Aunt Barb. "Or feeling. Whatever it is they do. She finds lost pets, and she talks to dead pets, and—"

"She talks to dead pets?" said Garth. "Why?"

"For their owners," said Aunt Barb. "You know, when owners miss them and want to find out if they're all right. Betty did that when her cat died. She went to see Ophelia, and Ophelia spoke to Yoda for her. And Yoda was fine. He said being dead was real nice, like being curled up on a rug next to a fire."

Weebie's tail twitched and he bent over. Garth realized the gerbil was doubled over with laughter.

Aunt Barb didn't notice. "Betty said Ophelia

can find out all kinds of things," she went on. "Like what's wrong if your pet is acting strange. Or disturbed. That's why we're seeing her. I want her to tell me what's wrong with Elvis. I think he misses Byron, but I'm not sure.

"I kind of miss him, too," she added. "Even if I did throw him out." For a moment her cheerful face looked sad. "But what's done is done," she said, more to herself than Garth.

She stood up. "Want another pancake?"

"No thanks," said Garth. "I'm stuffed." They watched Weebie eat a blueberry, and then Garth helped Aunt Barb do the dishes. Soon they were ready for their trip.

This time Garth was allowed to ride in the back of the truck with Elvis. There was a special seat back there, complete with a seat belt. There was a harness for Elvis, too.

"What about Weebie?" Garth's aunt asked him.

"I'll just keep him in my waist pack," said Garth. "He'll be fine."

"All right!" she said. "Let's rock and roll!" She put the truck into gear, and they were off.

But they didn't get very far. At the end of

the driveway they came face to face with an old green Chevy truck. Aunt Barb stopped and got out.

The driver of the green truck got out, too. He was a tall man with long blond hair, wearing jeans and cowboy boots.

Aunt Barb didn't look very happy to see him. "Byron," she said. "What brings you here?"

"Just wanted to see my old buddy, Elvis," said Byron. "I miss him. I'll bet he misses me, too." He came around to the back of the truck. Then he saw Garth.

"Well, who have we here?" he asked.

"This is my nephew, Garth," said Aunt Barb. "My sister's boy. He's visiting from up north."

"Hey there," said Byron, putting out his hand.

Garth shook it. Byron looked okay.

"Hey, Elvis!" said Byron. "How you doin', pal?" He unbuckled Elvis' harness, and the dog jumped out of the truck.

"Now Byron, can't you see we're just leaving?" said Aunt Barb.

"I'll just play with him for a minute," said

Byron. Before she could protest, he had taken off across the front yard with Elvis.

Aunt Barb tapped her foot while Byron threw a stick for her dog. "This is so typical," she said. "Just when everything is under control, he comes along and messes it up. Now we're going to be late. Just because Byron feels like playing. Life is just one big kiddy party to that man."

Garth didn't understand what was wrong with wanting to play, but he didn't say so. He could tell that Aunt Barb was pretty touchy about Byron.

At that moment Byron turned and caught them watching. "C'mon, pal," he said to Elvis. They ambled over to Aunt Barb's truck.

"He seems a little off to me," Byron said to Aunt Barb. "Not as frisky as he used to be." He patted Elvis' head. "Maybe he misses me."

"He's fine," snapped Aunt Barb.

"Sure you don't want him to come live with me?" said Byron teasingly. "He'd perk right up. Wouldn't you, Elvis? Bet you could use a little fun."

"Forget it." Aunt Barb's voice was cold. She

looked really angry. "He was mine before I met you, Byron. And he'll be mine long after you're gone."

"Okay, okay," said Byron. "Jeez."

"We have to go. We're late," said Aunt Barb, fastening Elvis' harness. Then she strode to the cab and got in. The door slammed and they drove away.

Garth waved good-bye to Byron, who just stood there watching them. "He seems like a nice guy," Garth said to Elvis. "I kind of feel sorry for him."

"Don't," said Elvis. "The whole time he lived with us, he acted like a lap dog. He just wanted to be petted and fed. Your aunt and I did all the work. He wouldn't even guard the house!"

Garth could see how that would be a problem. "So she kicked him out?"

"Yup. A few weeks ago she had to work the late shift. He said he'd make dinner. Of course he forgot. She came home at eleven, and he was drinking beer and watching television. Hadn't cooked a thing. He even forgot to feed me!"

"I know what that's like," squeaked Weebie,

poking his nose out of Garth's pack. "It's the worst."

"Anyway, that did it," Elvis went on. "She got angry. Then he got angry. Then she got even angrier. When he stormed out, she told him not to come back. And he didn't. Until today."

"Wow," said Garth, feeling glad he wasn't grown up yet.

"Maybe he'll change," said Weebie.

"Maybe I'll grow wings," said Elvis.

Garth unzipped his waist pack a little more so Weebie could stick his head out. Then he leaned back and let the wind make a mess of his hair.

"Wheee!" squeaked Weebie. "This is great!"

"I'll say," murmured Garth. It sure beat his parents' station wagon.

After a long ride through open country they came into a town. Its narrow, shady streets were lined with small wooden houses.

The house they pulled up to was big, though. And purple. It had towers, turrets, and stained-glass windows. Two tall bushes covered with giant purple flowers flanked the porch.

A sign on the lawn read, "OPHELIA LATOUCHE, ANIMAL PSYCHIC. BY APPOINTMENT ONLY. VISA, MASTERCARD, AMERICAN EXPRESS."

Aunt Barb got out of the truck and opened the tailgate for Garth and Elvis. "Here we are, guys," she said. "Let's see what Miss Latouche can tell us."

Garth tapped Weebie so he'd put his head back inside the waist pack.

"This should be very interesting," said Weebie.

CHAPTER FIVE

Vibrations

Before they had climbed the porch steps, the front door flew open. There stood a small, bony woman in a long purple dress. Her black hair was pulled back so tightly that her eyes slanted. Her unsmiling lips were deep purple. So were her fingernails. Rings set with purple stones flashed on all her fingers. Around her neck she wore a big silver cross, an even bigger Star of David, and a giant gold charm that looked like a wavy "E" turned backward.

"Don't come any closer," said the woman in a surprisingly deep voice. "I want to feel the vibrations."

They all stopped in their tracks. The woman's eyes closed and her nose wiggled. She sniffed loudly.

"I sense a great sadness here," she told them. "Come in."

They followed her through a shadowy hallway and into a parlor full of heavy carved furniture. The light in here was dim, too. It came from a pair of lamps with fringed shades and a group of purple candles flickering on a side table. Curtains, dusty purple ones, covered the windows. In the corner, perched on a branch in a glass case, was a bird. A stuffed crow.

Miss Latouche saw Garth staring at it. "That's Poe," she said. "Faithful companion. Dear, dear friend. When he died, I couldn't bear to part with him. Now he's with me always."

"Oh," said Garth, as if stuffing your friends when they died made perfect sense.

"Please sit down," said Miss Latouche, indicating three chairs arranged in a semi-circle. Garth and Aunt Barb sat, and Miss Latouche knelt suddenly, taking Elvis' face in both her hands. Moving her head slightly in a

circular motion, she gave him a long, searching look.

"Ah," she said. "Aha."

Then she settled next to Aunt Barb, keeping one hand on Elvis' head.

"Elvis hasn't—" Aunt Barb began.

"Quiet! Please!" commanded Miss Latouche. She closed her eyes.

"My voices are speaking," she intoned. "They say . . . pyramids. They say . . . Egypt! Yes!" She rocked back and forth. "Egypt in the time of Nefertiti!"

Garth heard a quiet little snort. That would be Weebie.

"I see a man," continued Miss Latouche. "A noble man. Noble, but sad. . . . Noble because he is of noble birth. Sad, because . . . he is in love. And the one he loves is far away. In . . . in Mesopotamia!"

Miss Latouche pressed her hand down on Elvis' head. He tried to wiggle away, but she held on.

"Yes!" she exclaimed. "That is why Elvis is sad. It is his past life! His unfulfilled love!" Her eyes flew open.

"This dog has a tragic, tragic past," she declared.

"Oh, would you give me just one small break!" squeaked Weebie. Garth tried not to smile.

"Wait!" said Miss Latouche. She blinked rapidly and then closed her eyes. "Something else is coming to me—another voice. An animal voice.

"Yes!" she went on. "I sense another animal here. It is interfering with my brain waves. It is . . . *hostile!*"

Garth was surprised. Maybe Miss Ophelia Latouche wasn't a total fake after all. He tapped his waist pack gently, hoping Weebie would get the hint and shut up.

For a moment the parlor was extremely quiet. Miss Latouche's nose twitched. She seemed to be trying to find Weebie. But he was quiet as a mouse. After a moment she spoke again.

"The hostile presence has been banished," she announced. "And good riddance to it!

"Now I will purify Elvis' aura," she said. She drew a bottle from her pocket and began massaging some kind of oil into Elvis' ears. It smelled terrible—like mothballs. Elvis groaned, but Miss Latouche ignored him.

"Begone, begone, dark karma, begone," she intoned. "Begone, begone," she repeated, picking up a little dish of black powder. She blew the powder into Elvis' face. "By the power vested in me by the state of Georgia and the United Psychic Workers' Union, I now pronounce you . . . free of your past life!"

Elvis sneezed.

"It's gone!" crowed Miss Latouche. "He's sneezing it away!"

Elvis sneezed again. "Will you get me out of here?" he groaned. "This is ridiculous!"

Miss Latouche turned to Aunt Barb. "He should be much happier now," she said. "And since we solved his problems so quickly, I'll give you a break on the price." She stood. "That'll be a hundred."

Aunt Barb pulled her wallet out of her jeans pocket. She handed the money over to Miss Latouche.

"Thanks," she said, a little doubtfully.

"A pleasure," said Miss Latouche. She led

them all to the door. "Good-bye and good karma," she said to Elvis.

Elvis just looked at her. Garth could tell the dog had lost all patience. "C'mon, guy," he said, hurrying Elvis down the front steps. "Let's go."

Miss Latouche's door slammed shut and Aunt Barb shook her head. "Am I crazy, or was that a total waste of money?" she asked.

"Phonus balonus!" squeaked Weebie.

"Total," said Garth.

The Yellow Balloon

The next day Aunt Barb woke Garth at ten. "Up and at 'em, nephew," she said. "We've got a game today, remember?"

"All *right!*" murmured Garth sleepily. He definitely remembered about the game. The Braves were playing the Phillies today. It should be awesome.

While they ate breakfast, Elvis lay under the table, sighing. "Maybe we should take Elvis with us," said Aunt Barb. "He looks so blue, I hate to leave him alone. That animal psychic didn't do him any good, did she?"

"Animal psycho, you mean!" squeaked Weebie from behind Garth's cereal bowl.

"She made him worse!"

Weebie was right, thought Garth. Elvis *was* worse after seeing Miss Latouche. He'd hardly said a word since the trip, and this morning he wasn't even begging for pancakes, the way he usually did.

Garth felt a pang of guilt. He and Weebie had promised to help Elvis. But so far, what had they done? Nothing.

A few hours later they were in the truck, chugging down the highway. Elvis was in back, as usual. After a few miles Garth decided to sound his aunt out a little.

"Aunt Barb," he said, "do you think Elvis could ever sing the anthem at a Braves game?" He tried to sound casual.

His aunt looked startled. "Elvis? You mean my *dog* Elvis?"

"Sure. He's great at it, right?"

She smiled. "Well, sure, but he's just a dog. Dogs don't sing 'The Star-Spangled Banner.' Not to open a game, anyway. Big stars do."

"Oh," said Garth. "Is anyone singing today?"

"I think it's Tammy Weevilcross," said Aunt

Barb. "The country singer? She's got a big hit right now—'Don't Call Me Long Distance, Just Fax Me Your Love.' "

Hearing some celebrity sing the anthem would make Elvis feel even worse, thought Garth. For the rest of the trip he didn't say much. Neither did Weebie.

When they got to the stadium, Aunt Barb drove around the lot until she found a place under a tree, so Elvis would be in the shade. They climbed out of the truck, and she filled his water bowl.

"We'll be back soon, sweetheart," she promised, giving him a pat.

" 'Bye, Elvis," said Garth.

"Don't mind me," whined Elvis. "I'll just sit out here while some tone-deaf celebrity murders the anthem." He put his head down on his paws.

"He's in bad shape," squeaked Weebie.

"I know," said Garth, following Aunt Barb out of the lot. Soon they were part of the crowd climbing the steps to the stadium. They reached the top, where a great big bronze statue of Hank Aaron stood. The statue was awesome, and for a little while it made Garth forget about Elvis' problems.

Then they walked through the ticket gate and heard an announcement that Tammy Weevilcross wouldn't be singing that day. She had a sore throat.

"Too bad," said Aunt Barb. "Would've been fun to hear her."

But Garth felt a jolt of excitement. If Tammy Weevilcross wasn't singing, maybe Elvis could! Weebie started rustling hard inside Garth's waist pack.

"We've got to talk!" he squeaked, as if he'd read Garth's mind.

Garth fell behind his aunt a little. "Okay," he whispered. The crowd was so noisy that Aunt Barb didn't hear him. She was heading past the front office and up a ramp, along with everybody else. But when they reached the ladies' room, she stopped.

"Would you mind waiting for just a minute?" she asked Garth.

"Take your time," he replied. As soon as she went inside, he moved over to a bank of pay phones. Checking to make sure that nobody was watching, he pulled Weebie out of his pack

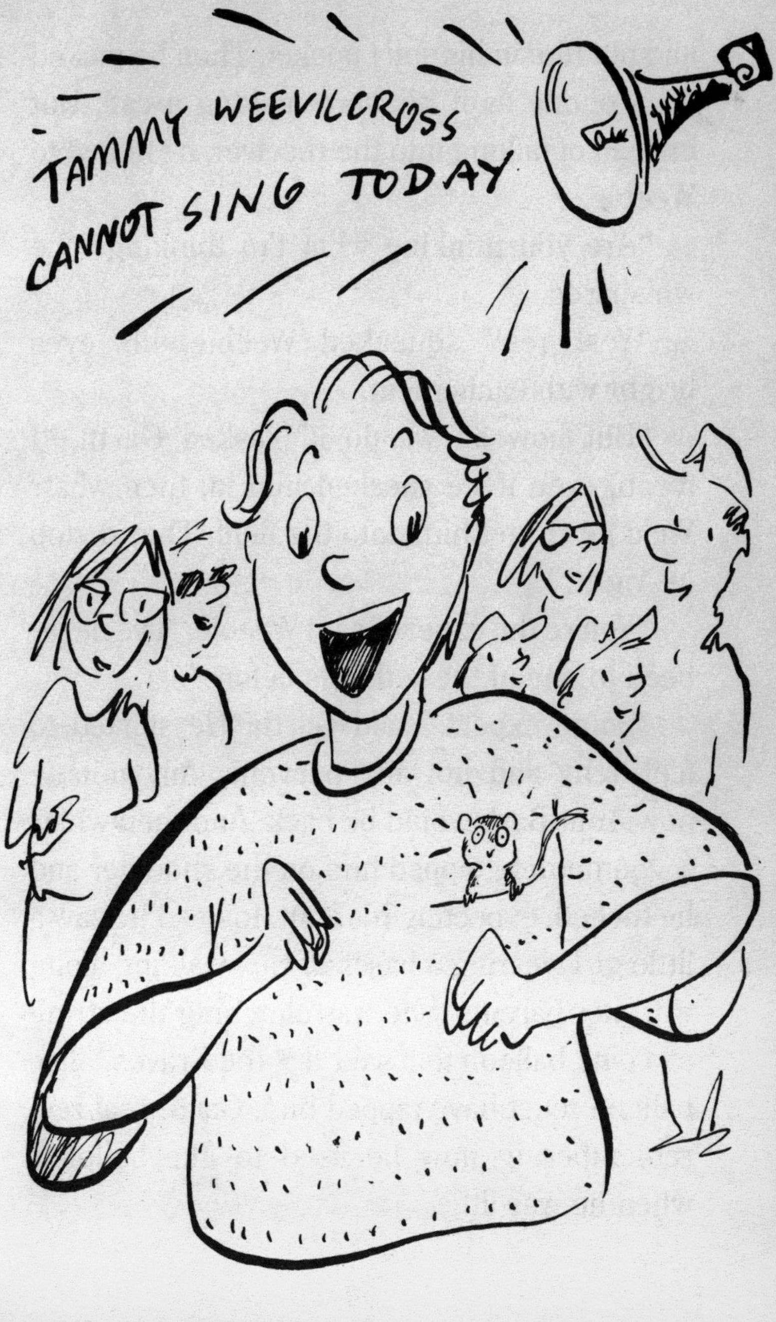
TAMMY WEEVILCROSS CANNOT SING TODAY

and put him in his shirt pocket. Then he picked up a phone as if he were making a call. But instead of talking into the receiver, he talked to Weebie.

"Are you thinking what I'm thinking?" he whispered.

"Yes! Yes!" squeaked Weebie, his eyes bright with excitement.

"But how do we do it?" asked Garth. "I mean, even if we sneaked him in, then what? We'd never get him onto the field. They'd stop us, right?"

"You're the expert," said Weebie. "I've never been to one of these things before."

"Some expert," said Garth. He started to feel itchy and hot and nervous. Any minute now Aunt Barb would be back. And then what?

Something tapped him on the shoulder and he turned, expecting his aunt. Instead he saw a little girl wearing a baseball cap, walking along with her parents. She was clutching the string of a pink balloon that said "I ♥ the Braves." The balloon must have tapped him, Garth realized, remembering how he used to like balloons when he was little.

But not with dumb heart signs on them, that was for sure.

Then, as he watched the balloon bob away through the crowd, an idea began to take shape in Garth's mind. He looked back toward the stadium entrance. A guy with long hair was selling balloons right near the gate.

"That's it!" said Garth. "Weeb, listen to this!"

He had just finished telling Weebie about his idea when he felt another tap on his shoulder. He whirled around. This time it was his aunt.

"Who're you calling, honey?" she asked.

"Uh, nobody," stammered Garth, hanging up the phone quickly. "But I do, uh, have to go to the men's room," he said, feeling his face get red. He was a terrible liar—he always blushed.

"Sure," said his aunt. "I'll wait for you."

Garth's mind raced. He couldn't do anything if Aunt Barb stuck around. "Do you, uh, mind if I walk around a little before the game?" he asked her. "I thought I might buy a souvenir or something."

"Course not," she said. "Just hang on to this." She handed him his ticket stub. "You can find your way to the upper level, right?"

"Sure," said Garth. "And thanks." He smiled at her gratefully.

"No big deal." She smiled back. "Just remember to come up by two, okay? That's when the game starts."

He nodded and walked into the men's room. A second later he was out again, heading back toward the stadium entrance.

The balloon vendor was young, wearing ripped jeans and a tie-dyed shirt. His long hair was blond—except for a crew-cut patch in front that was bright purple.

"Can I get a balloon?" Garth asked him.

"Sure, man. What color?"

Garth thought about it. "Yellow would be best," he said.

"Yellow it is," said the vendor, untangling one from the bunch. "That'll be one twenty-five."

Garth dug around in his pocket. All he had was change. He took it out and counted it: "A dollar, a dollar ten, a dollar fifteen, a dollar seventeen . . ." That was it: a dollar seventeen.

"Hey, no sweat, man," said the balloon

seller. "This will be, like, my good deed for the day. Here." He handed Garth the balloon.

"Thanks!" Garth took the balloon and raced to the parking lot. Elvis was lying in the back of the truck with his head on his paws.

"Game over so soon?" he asked glumly.

"Elvis! This is it!" squeaked Weebie from Garth's shirt pocket.

Elvis lifted an eyebrow. "What?"

"Your chance to sing!" said Garth. He was a little out of breath. And he knew they had to hurry. His watch said 1:45.

"What do you mean?" asked Elvis. "Isn't there some human singing?" His voice was bitter.

"She's sick!" squeaked Weebie.

"We figure you can take her place," said Garth. "But we've got to hurry."

Elvis saw that Garth was serious. "Undo me!" he barked.

Garth unfastened his harness, and Elvis bounded out of the truck. He jumped up on Garth's chest, wagging his tail furiously. "Is it true?" he demanded. "Can I really sing? Really?" Then he noticed the yellow balloon. "What's that for?" he asked.

"It's part of the plan," said Garth. "Which reminds me." With a felt-tip pen he began to write on the balloon—very carefully, so he wouldn't pop it.

When he had finished, he tied the string to Elvis' collar and stepped back to take a look. "Great," he said. "It looks great. Really."

"I feel like a fool!" complained Elvis.

"I know," said Garth. "But it's for a really good cause."

"I think you look cute," said Weebie slyly.

The balloon bobbed above Elvis' head. It said, MY NAME IS ELVIS, AND I WANT TO SING!

"Okay. Let's go," said Garth.

Holding the balloon under his arm, he flashed his ticket stub and hustled through the turnstile, praying nobody would stop him.

Nobody did.

Just beyond the entrance was the place he was looking for—the front office. Through a glass panel in the door he could see a room full of desks and people, and a big clock on the wall that said 1:51.

Garth knelt down to Elvis. "You know what to do, don't you?" he said.

"I do," said Elvis, yawning nervously.

"Go for it!" squeaked Weebie. "You'll be great! You'll make history!"

Garth opened the door and pushed Elvis into the office. Once he was inside, the balloon rose up above him, where everyone could see it.

At first no one did. In these last few minutes before the game, the room was loud and busy— everyone was either talking on the phone or rushing somewhere. It took a while for anyone to notice a hound dog with a yellow balloon attached to his collar.

Then it happened. A woman sitting at a desk near the door saw him. "Well, fan my brow!" she exclaimed. She got up and walked over to Elvis, who was sitting patiently, waiting for attention.

When she read the message on the balloon, her penciled eyebrows flew up. "Hey, you guys!" she called to the others. "Come and look at this!"

A few people walked over. There was a burst of surprised laughter as more people joined them and read the balloon. Pretty soon Elvis was surrounded by a small crowd.

"Can you really sing, sugar?" a woman asked him.

He wagged his tail so it swished on the floor.

A man wearing a short-sleeved shirt and a tie with baseballs on it came over to see Elvis. "Well, well," he said, smiling. "Let's see what he can do. Pipe down, everyone."

He turned to the dog. "Sing, Elvis, sing!" he said.

Elvis sat up very tall and closed his eyes. He threw his head back. "Ow-ow-ow ow ow *owwww*—" he sang.

With the first slow, deep notes of the song came a gasp of surprise, as people recognized the anthem.

Then, except for his sweet, measured, almost mournful singing, there was absolute silence. Garth felt goose bumps.

At the end pandemonium broke loose. "Incredible!"

"He's great!"

"Let's get him to open the game! Today!"

"Somebody call Ted!"

As people grabbed telephones, a man in a security guard's uniform spotted Garth,

who was standing in the doorway.

"Hey, kid! Is that your dog?" he asked.

Garth stepped into the room. "Well, actually, he's my aunt's," he told the guard.

"Did you put the balloon on him?"

Garth looked down, embarrassed. "Me and a friend."

"Brilliant!" said the man in the baseball tie. "Fantastic!"

"Listen, son," said an older man holding an unlit cigar, "do you think this dog could sing the anthem before the game today?"

Garth smiled. It was a question he was really happy to answer. "I know he could," he said.

Elvis Sings

A little while later, as he and Elvis were led from the office down to the field level, Garth remembered his aunt. She'd be worrying about him—it was 2:05. Then he almost kicked himself. Worried! In a few minutes she'd see Elvis out on the field, opening the game!

"Son, do you think you ought to walk him out to centerfield?" asked the man with the cigar as they got out of the service elevator.

"You want me to go with him?" asked Garth, a little stunned.

"Might be a good idea," said the man. "In case he gets confused or scared when he's supposed to sing."

"Fat chance," squeaked Weebie, who was wiggling around in Garth's shirt pocket.

Then they were at the entrance to the field. Garth had never seen so many people in his life. Elvis looked up at him and gave a tiny whine.

Garth squatted down so they were face to face. "You okay?" he asked.

"I'm all right," said Elvis. "Just a little stage fright."

"What's wrong?" said the man with the cigar. "Stage fright?"

"He's fine," said Garth. He patted Elvis' head. "You'll knock 'em dead," he told the dog.

As they started out across the immense bright-green field, an announcer's voice boomed over the sound system.

"Folks, we have a real treat for you," said the announcer. "There's someone very special with us today to sing the national anthem. His name is Elvis."

A few women screamed when they heard the name. But as Garth and Elvis walked up to home plate, a confused murmur swept the stadium.

Garth patted Elvis' head. "Ready, guy?" he asked softly.

Elvis looked up at him, eyes glowing. Then he sat, lifted his head, and began to sing.

His voice echoed through the stadium, sounding as deep and sweet and warm as some enchanted stringed instrument. Garth had never heard the anthem sung with such emotion. He had never heard it sound so beautiful. When Elvis finished, drawing out the last note so the air seemed to vibrate with its sound, the audience was silent for a long time.

Then it went wild.

Suddenly the entire crowd was on its feet, stamping, clapping, cheering, and whistling. "El-*vis!* El-*vis!* El-*vis!*" they chanted.

Elvis bowed his head, wagging his tail furiously.

Then he looked up at Garth and Weebie. "This is the happiest moment of my life," he said.

CHAPTER EIGHT

Frisky Again

Aunt Barb was so excited about Elvis that she didn't even care that the Braves had lost the game. "Whooo-*weee!*" she said for about the fifteenth time as they drove home. "That was amazing! Nephew Garth, you are just the living end! I never believed for a second that Elvis could sing at a Braves game. But you did! And you made it happen!"

Garth did feel pretty pleased with himself.

"Did you hear those people screaming?" she went on. "They just loved him!"

"Of course they loved him," said Weebie, poking his head out of Garth's pocket. "He's good."

"They did love me," sighed Elvis happily. "I mean, I know I'm supposed to be modest, but I felt it. And it was the best."

"I wonder what Elvis is mumbling and grumbling about?" said Aunt Barb. "Maybe it's that hot dog I fed him after the game."

Garth patted Elvis' head. "He's just happy," he said.

When they got to Aunt Barb's house, three cars were parked in the front yard—a shiny new black Jeep, a beige-and-white Nash Rambler, and a rusty old red Jaguar.

"Well, well," said Aunt Barb. "Arthur, Betty, and Attila are here." They walked into the house, and Aunt Barb's friends jumped up, whooping and whistling their congratulations. Everybody hugged everybody else. Then they all hugged Elvis. Attila kissed him on the nose.

"You are truly the king!" he shouted. "I worship at your feet!"

In the commotion the phone rang and Aunt Barb answered it. "Yes? Yes, I am," she said, motioning for everyone to quiet down. "Yes, well, he is free. Next Thursday? I think so. Sure." She began to scribble on the back of an envelope. "He's a busy dog, though. What? A manager? No, he doesn't have a manager. Yet. Okay, see you then."

She hung up the phone. "That was a record company in New York," she told them, her eyes wide. "They want to take me and Elvis out to lunch. They want to give him a recording contract."

"Holy cow!" said Garth.

Elvis did a little spin around the room, wagging his tail. "I knew it! I knew it!" he said.

"Well, would you just look at him," said Aunt Barb. "He's his old self again. Frisky! Almost as if he knows what's happening." She knelt down and hugged Elvis again. "This was what you needed, wasn't it?" she said. "Ancient Egypt, my foot!"

"My four feet!" cried Weebie. "With toenail polish on!"

The phone rang again, and again Aunt Barb answered it. "Yes. Yes," she said. "For TV tonight? Really. Well, I guess I could give you an interview. An hour from now? Sure. Off Route 103, a mile and a half down Walston Road. Look for a sunflower over the mailbox.

Right. Okay! See you later."

She put down the phone. "Whoo-*weee*!" she exclaimed. "CNN!"

"I hate to interrupt the excitement," said Attila, opening the refrigerator. "But if they're coming in an hour, maybe we should rustle up something to eat."

"Rustle away, Attila," said Aunt Barb. "But it won't do much good. The fridge is empty. Somehow shopping escaped my mind this afternoon."

"We have dessert," said Betty. "I brought Twinkies."

"Ooo! I love Twinkies," squeaked Weebie.

There was a soft knock on the screen door. "Hello?" called a man's voice.

It was Byron. He was carrying two big brown supermarket bags.

"Well, come on the heck in, Byron," said Aunt Barb. "I'm in such a good mood right now, I can't even be mad at you."

Byron looked surprised. "How come?"

"Didn't you watch the game today?" asked Betty.

"Nope."

"So you don't know about Elvis," said Arthur.

"Nope," said Byron. "I came by earlier, but nobody was home. Y'all been to the game?"

"I'll say," said Aunt Barb. Then she told Byron about Elvis.

"I always knew this pup was special," said Byron, grinning. "I'm proud of him!"

"Why don't you put those bags down, Byron?" said Arthur. "They look heavy."

"What brings you here anyhow?" Aunt Barb asked him.

"Well," said Byron slowly, "I joined this men's group. Just a bunch of guys. We're all trying to be more sensitive."

"How?" asked Aunt Barb.

"Well, we—uh—we bang on drums. And we hug each other. We express our feelings."

Aunt Barb's mouth dropped open, but she didn't say anything.

"And I got this book," Byron went on. He pulled a dog-eared paperback out of his pocket. The book's title was *How to Be a Better Boyfriend*. "Basically it's about how I was a jerk. So what I did was, I went to the

Friendly Mart and bought stuff to make you a nice dinner. And wine, too."

Aunt Barb blinked. "Well, Byron," she said softly. "Maybe you're not a total loser after all." She turned to Garth and the others. "I think Byron and I need to talk while he makes dinner," she said.

"Pardon me for asking," said Attila, "but will there be enough for us, too?"

"Sure thing," said Byron.

They all filed out onto the porch. Garth settled on a step, with Weebie on his knee. Arthur, Betty, and Attila sat on the porch swing. The late-afternoon light was soft and golden, and they admired it in silence for a while. Then Elvis bounded up and ran around the yard chasing a butterfly.

"Will you look at him go?" asked Betty.

"He's a different dog," said Arthur.

"He's the king!" said Attila.

They sat there until the light went from pink-orange to velvety gray. Crickets started chirping, and the delicious smell of homemade spaghetti sauce wafted out of the kitchen.

Elvis sat with his head on Garth's lap,

getting his ears scratched.

"Things are going to be a lot better around here from now on," said Weebie.

Garth flew home a week later. His parents were at the airport when he landed. They were tan, smiling, and standing with their arms around each other.

"Garth, honey!" called his mother, rushing over to hug him.

His father, beaming, tousled his hair.

"Careful, don't squish Weebie," said Garth.

"Oh, sorry," said his mother. She looked at Weebie's little head sticking out of the waist pack. "Hi, Weebie," she said.

"Hi, Garth's mom," squeaked Weebie.

"Did you have a good time in Bermuda?" Garth asked his parents.

"We had a great time," said his mother.

"Wonderful," said his father.

"And how about you?" asked his mother. "Did you have a good time with your aunt Barb?"

"*Really* good," said Garth.

His father picked up Garth's duffel, and they walked down the hallway toward the exit. "So," said his mother, falling into step with him, "does Barb still have that frisky dog?"

"She sure does," said Garth. "She sure does."